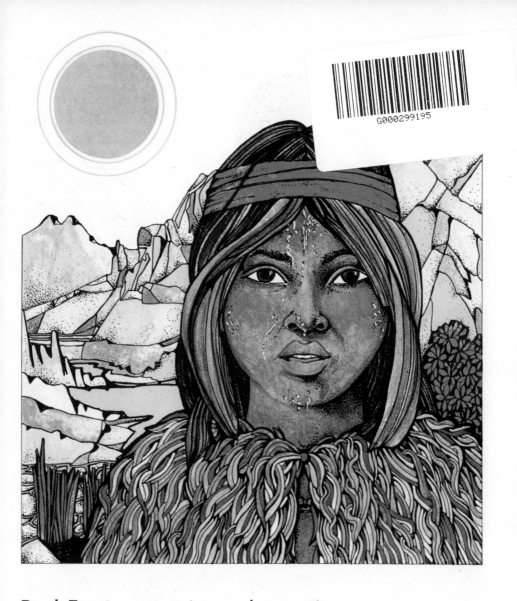

Red Foal went along the trail.
It was a long road in the hills.
The sun made Red Foal feel very hot.
"I don't need my buffalo coat," he said.
"I shall take it off."

So, he put the coat under his arm
and went on his way.
The road was long and the sun was hot.
Red Foal became hotter and hotter.
"This coat is too big a load," he said.
"I will give it away."

2

"This big rock must be hot," said Red Foal.
"My coat will shelter it from the sun.
 It will be like a cloak."
 So he put his coat over the rock,
 and went on his way.

But soon black clouds filled the sky.
They hid the sun and were full of rain.
The hills became darker and darker.
Red Foal wished he had kept his coat.

A goat was sitting by the trail.
"The clouds are black," it said.
"They are full of rain.
You have no coat, Red Foal.
You will get soaked to the skin."

"I gave my coat to a rock," said the boy.
"A rock has no need of a coat," said the goat.
"Soon it will rain and you will get soaked.
Let me run back and fetch your coat."

6

Red Foal looked up at the sky.
It was full of rain clouds.
There was no sun to be seen,
and he was no longer hot.
"Yes," he said. "Run back down the road,
and bring me my buffalo coat."

The goat ran back to the rock.
He snatched the coat from its back,
and ran back to the boy.
He was just in time.
It began to rain.

8

As they set off along the road,
there was a big din.
It was the big rock rumbling, grumbling
and tumbling after them.
"Give back my buffalo coat," it moaned.
"When a thing is given, it is given.
You cannot take it back.
Give back my buffalo coat."

Then, all the rocks on the trail moaned too.
"Give it back, give it back.
When a thing is given, it is given.
You cannot take it back.
Give back the buffalo coat."

Red Foal was afraid.
He began to run and the goat ran too.
They ran up hills and down hills.
But the big rock still rumbled, grumbled
and tumbled after them.

"You bad little boy," groaned the rock.
"Give back my buffalo coat.
When a thing is given, it is given."
Then, all the rocks on the trail groaned too.
"You bad little boy. Give back the coat."

But still the rain came down.
So, Red Foal clung to his coat.
"No! No!" he cried.
"If I give back this coat,
  I shall get soaked to the skin."
Then the goat found a hole and cried,
"Jump in and hide."

The goat and Red Foal jumped into the hole.
The rock tried to jump in too.
But it was much too big.
So it sat on the hole and groaned,
"I shall sit on this hole till I get my coat.
Or I shall sit here for ever."

14

"It's dark in this hole," said the goat.
"Soon we shall be hungry.
 The big rock will not go away
 unless you give back the coat.
 It will sit on this hole for ever.
 So give back the coat, and we shall be free."

"No, I will not," said Red Foal.
"You are only a goat.
You give your coat to the rock."
"My coat is stuck to my skin," said the goat.
"I cannot get it off."

16

Then the goat began to dig a tunnel.
It dug and scraped and scratched away.
After a while it crept back to the boy.
"Sh! Sh! little Red Foal.
Softly, softly, we can creep away."

They crept to the end of the tunnel.
And, away from the hole, they ran
softly on tiptoe under the trees.
"We shall soon be at the river.
Then we shall be safe," panted the goat.
18

But Red Foal trod on a pebble.

"Give back the coat," it softly moaned.

The pebble tapped a little stone.

"Give back the coat," the little stone moaned.

The little stone knocked a big stone.

"Give back the coat," the big stone groaned.

The big stone bumped a little rock.

"Give back the coat," the little rock groaned.

Soon all the pebbles, stones and rocks
were moaning and groaning.
"Give it back! Give it back!
When a thing is given, it is given."
This made the big rock wake up
and rumble off again
after Red Foal and the goat.

"I am afraid," panted the goat.
"The rain has stopped so drop the coat.
 The rock will pick it up and go home."
"No! No!" panted little Red Foal.
"I will never give up the coat."
"Then we must cross the river,"
 gasped the goat.
"We need a boat and boatman."
 But there was no boat and boatman.
 So Red Foal cried, "I will swim across.
 I can swim, but the big rock will sink."

Red Foal was boasting, but he was still afraid.
He was so afraid he forgot the goat.
He was so afraid he forgot the coat.
"I cannot swim in a coat," he cried.
So he took off the coat and jumped in the river.

22

The goat did not jump in the river.
It just sat on the bank under an oak tree,
and waited for the big rock to rumble up.
"Stop moaning and groaning," said the goat.
"Here is the buffalo coat.
So sit and rest under this oak tree."

The big rock did as it was told.
"It's cool by the river," it moaned.
"It's so cool I shall stay here for ever.
But I must not get a chill, little goat.
So put the coat over me like a cloak."
The goat did as it was told.
It put the buffalo coat over the rock,
and it, too, crept under the coat,
and fell fast asleep.